Funny Fish

Cynthia Rider • Alex Brychta

OXFORD
UNIVERSITY PRESS

Mum Dad Biff

Chip Kipper Floppy

Kipper was fishing.

He got a hat.

Biff was fishing.

She got a crab.

Chip was fishing.

He got an octopus!

Mum was fishing.

She got a bucket.

Dad was fishing.

He got a boot.

SPLASH!

Floppy got a fish!

Think about the story

Why do you
think Floppy fell
into the water?

Who do you
think caught the
funniest fish?

What would you do
if you caught a big crab,
like Biff?

Floppy's fish
lives in the sea.
Where else do
fish live?

Tangled lines

Follow the lines to see who gets the fish.

Useful common words repeated in this story and other books at Level 1.

a got he she was

Names in this story: Mum Dad Biff Chip Kipper Floppy